Chester

by ~~Mélanie Watt~~ Chester

DEAR admirers,

Due to an OVERWHELMING amount of fan mail, I, Chester, am back with an amazing, brilliant, SMART, SUPER new book!

C.

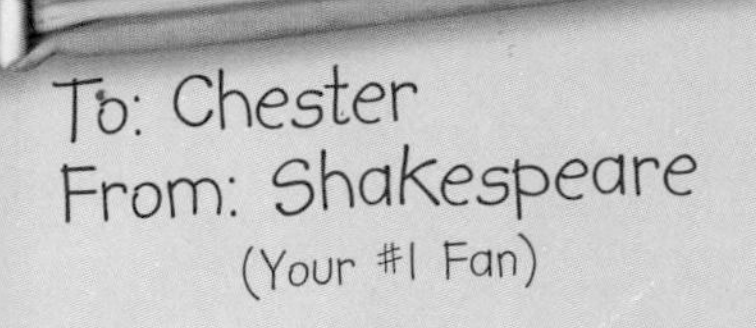

Dear Readers,

Please forgive Chester. He's forgotten to mention that he wrote all those fan letters himself.

M.W.

For my sister,
Valérie ... who is much nicer than me.
But, more importantly, I would like to thank CHESTER, the star of this book, for being kind enough to take time off from his busy schedule to be in this sequel.
I OWE him BIG time!!!

Kids Can Press acknowledges the financial support of the Government of Ontario, through the Ontario Media Development Corporation's Ontario Book Initiative; the Ontario Arts Council; the Canada Council for the Arts; and the Government of Canada, through the BPIDP, for our publishing activity.

Published in Canada by
Kids Can Press Ltd.
29 Birch Avenue
Toronto, ON M4V 1E2

Published in the U.S. by
Kids Can Press Ltd.
2250 Military Road
Tonawanda, NY 14150

www.kidscanpress.com

Kids Can Press is a Corus™ Entertainment company

The artwork in this book was rendered in pencil and watercolor and was assembled digitally.

The text is set in Carnation and Kidprint.

Edited by Tara Walker
Designed by Mélanie Watt
Author photo by Tiness
Printed and bound in Singapore

The paper used to print this book was produced with elemental chlorine-free pulp, harvested from managed sustainable forests.

This book is smyth sewn casebound.

CM 08 0 9 8 7 6 5 4 3 2 1

LIBRARY AND ARCHIVES CANADA CATALOGUING IN PUBLICATION

WATT, MÉLANIE, 1975
CHESTER'S BACK! / WRITTEN AND ILLUSTRATED BY MÉLANIE WATT.

SEQUEL TO: CHESTER.
AGES 4 TO 8.
ISBN 978-1-55453-287-2

I. TITLE.

PS8645.A884C44 2008 jC813'.6 C2007-907014-0

Chester's Back!

Written and illustrated by Mélanie Watt's hero

KIDS CAN PRESS

A long time ago, in a faraway land,
lived a cat named Chester.

I SAID...

A long time ago, in a faraway land, lived a cat named Chester.

NOT ready yet!

A long time ago ...

CHESTER, not THAT long ago!

BORING!

CAVE CAT take over!
Ooga Chugga Ooga Chugga!

A long, long,
long, long, long,
long time ago,
in a faraway
CAVE, lived
CHESTER.

He was famous!
He invented
the WHEEL!

© CHESTER for story and cave drawings and the wheel
CHESTER's invention

Little did the cave cat know that
soon he would become extinct!

TAKE 4
Now, Chester, let's try this again.
A long time ago, in a faraway land,
lived a … stinky dinosaur in need
of a major breath mint!
Chester, get out from behind there!
Nope, THIS side looks
WAY better!
CHESTER! CUT IT OUT!!!

IF YOU SAY SO...
Ladies and Gentlemen,
I, the GREAT
CHESTERDINI,
will now attempt
to saw this boring
drawing in half!!!
Chester ...
Don't do it!

KABOOM!!!!!!!
Meet Mélanie,
the bearded
lady!

THAT'S IT, CHESTER!!!

No more clowning around!

It's time for your disappearing act!

Mélanie Watt seeks replacement
to play the role of CHESTER

36
35
34
31
30
29
17
21
15
14
12
9
11
Number 1,
please step into
the story.

Pffff!
Bunch of copycats!

TAKE 5

A long time ago, in a faraway land, lived a cat named Chester.

Wait a minute!

Chester, step away from the new Chester!

1

This page ain't BIG enough for the BOTH of us!

I'm outta here!!!
1

Chester, I give up!
WHAT DO YOU WANT???

GLAD YOU ASKED!
I want a story that takes place in a LONG limousine.

I want GIANT billboards with MY face on them all over the CITY!

He's unbelievable!

AND, since I'm VERY famous, I demand jellybeans but ONLY the red ones. AND... oh yes, my name written in lights! And when I arrive on the red carpet, I want everyone to see I'm a BIG STAR!!!

Is that it?

Mmm... and a bell so that I can ring for Mouse anytime I need something.

Fine, Chester.

Hmm... make that SIR Chester.

Okay, SIR...
You asked for it!

Not long ago, in a big city somewhere,
a VERY famous cat named Sir Chester
arrived in a long, long, long limousine
filled with red jellybeans.
Everyone was excited to see ...

SIR
CHESTER
SIR CHESTER
NOW ARRIVING:
SIR CHESTER

... the BIG STAR!
THE WORLDWIDE NEWS
SIR CHESTER TURNS HEADS IN FUNNY-LOOKING STAR OUTFIT
WHAT WAS THIS CAT THINKING?

That's NOT what I had in mind.

WANTED

Famous CAT seeks talented creator
to replace Mélanie Watt for next picture book!!!

REWARD

500 gazillion red jellybeans